MY SILENT SISTER
and her
RUSTY CAGE

CHRISTOPHER J. WEEKS

ISBN: 978-1-954771-07-9

Published in the United States of America

www.christopherjweeks.com

∞∞∞∞

However, as it is written:
"What no eye has seen, what no ear has heard,
and what no human mind has conceived"—
the things God has prepared for those who love him—

(1 Corinthians 2:9)

∞∞∞∞

PART ONE

Life on this terrestrial plain comes down to numbers.

When you pause to think about the magnitude of the numbers that go into making a single human body, the totals are quite staggering: 37 trillion cells, each containing over 3 billion DNA building blocks that compose 23 pairs of chromosomes determine a person's specific genetic code. In those 23 pairs, there are up to 20,000 genetic strands, forming into various sequences of proteins, that make you, you.

Scientists tell us that out of all the numbers, there is a fifty-percent difference in the genetic material that keeps you from being a fly. A mere six-percent variation keeps you from swinging in the trees like a monkey. And only one-percent deviation takes you from looking and acting just like me. Phew, don't you feel lucky, you are a hair's breadth away from scratching your belly and howling at the moon.

Numbers matter, small, tiny, microscopic numbers matter, a lot.

Take my sister Laura Lee. From personal experience she has found out that if there is less than a one-thousandth of one-percent difference in the genetic structure of the human body, it will drastically alter your world. In her specific case, a random spontaneous mutation occurred on only eight hot-spots of one small portion of the DNA on one of her X-chromosomes, which caused her body to severely malfunction. A few neurological shorts which were found in her cellular circuitry has caused my sister's body to wage war against herself. The body she has been born into has become a rusty immovable cage that has bound her soul in a prison of silence.

⣿⣿⣿⣿

"You wired me awake

And hit me with a hand of broken nails

You tied my lead and pulled my chain."

(Rusty Cage, Soundgarden)

⣿⣿⣿⣿

"Mom, Laura won't stop screaming! I'm trying to watch my show and she is doing that crazy shaking and drooling and shrieking thing again." Looking over at my sister she had both of her bony hands clamped together in front of her small framed body squeezing tight. As if she was fighting an invisible foe, there she sat on the couch rapidly rocking back and forth with a look of pinched anguish on the front of her face. Her small mouth was twisted in a crooked grin while a large string of drool hung from her bottom lip.

"Laura, stop it!" I yelled. "Mom, she is drooling all over the couch...it is gross!" But my sister was lost in her own world, still rocking away with hands clenched, white-knuckled. Her intense eyes were focused on nothing discernible staring out straight with a blank cross-eyed expression. I was sitting only 3 feet away and my poor sister couldn't even acknowledge my presence. I didn't seem to exist in her world, at least I couldn't tell if I did.

My mom threw a stained, old yellow towel at me and told me to wipe her chin. The anger I felt at Laura's screaming quickly subsided as I soaked up the small splashes of spittle that fell on her bare arm and edge of the couch that she was sitting on. I knew her screaming wasn't her fault. She was not to blame, it was that rotten disease.

$\infty\infty\infty$

Somewhere around the age of 16 months, my sister Laura Lee's brain stopped working. For her whole first year of life she was like any other baby. She would smile at my mom's face, laugh at my dad's tickling, and grab for the same toys her baby brother Donny wanted. And boy did she love Mary Poppins! My dad would often pull out a 33 RPM vinyl record which contained all the musical numbers from the movie and when he played "I Love to Laugh" Laura would stop everything she was doing and smile, grin and hold up her chubby little fist in glee.

And then, without warning, without reason, some of the wirings in her body started shorting out. This lovely child who was born in New Orleans—we pronounced her name as Lara because my mom said she was the only southern bell in the family—stopped responding to the world around her. Her mind went blank and her body started revolting against nature with terrifying violence. Her tender little frame was rendered helpless to oncoming bouts of random seizures, violent rocking and a continual wringing of her hands.

As the symptoms increased, my mom and dad desperately looked for help. Taking her to numerous doctors and neurologists, they searched for answers. Any answers. But none could be given. For two grueling years, my parents made hundreds of calls, drove to various hospitals, and looked for any solution to help find a cure for their small fragile daughter.

But none could be found.

Day after day my sweet sister slipped deeper and deeper into her rusty cage. A prisoner to a body that no longer worked.

◦◦◦◦

"You have got to be kidding me! You want me to stay home every other day this summer to take care of Laura? But mom, I want to play baseball and go to the pool. That isn't fair."

My mom looked up from the table after feeding Laura Lee another large spoonful of strawberry jello and said, "You know what isn't fair? Having a life like Laura's!" After wiping a red trickle of slobber from my sister's chin with a dish towel my mom continued, "She will never go to the pool, drive a car, or have her friends over. And plus, your sister Stephanie is going to split the time with you."

"But Mom, Laura bites my fingers when I try to feed her!" I said with disgust.

This caused my mom to laugh with a soft chuckle, "Well Chris, you deserve it. It probably is her way to get back at you for always having a bad attitude about feeding her. I would guess that she hates the thought of having her little brother care for her. Isn't that right, Laura?" Just at that moment, my sister let out a blast of air with chunks of uneaten red jello flying across the plastic cover on the kitchen table. "Yep, Laura, I agree. Little Chrissy is not the best company, is he?"

With my arms crossed, I stomped up the stairs to go to my room.

∞∞∞

Twenty years. That is how long it took to finally get a diagnosis. It came from my brother Don. I will never forget the day he came rushing into the kitchen to tell my mom and dad how he met a little girl that was just like Laura. While he was at work a mother came strolling into the lobby where his office was and she was pushing her small daughter in a wheelchair.

The girl was wringing her hands, rocking back and forth and had a distant stare just like Laura.

He went up to the lady and said, "She looks like my sister! How old is she?" The lady replied that she was eight years old. My brother said his sister Laura was twenty.

"That is impossible!" Cried the distraught woman. "My daughter has Rett syndrome and there are very few known cases of someone living past the age of seventeen with Retts."

My brother insisted. "I'm telling you, my sister has the same symptoms and the same faraway look." The mother clearly didn't want to talk. My brother then asked her, "Would you like to meet my sister, we don't live too far away?"

Wiping a flow of warm tears away with her sleeve, she said, "No, I couldn't bear it. It is hard enough just trying to take care of an eight-year-old with Retts, I couldn't imagine what a twenty-year-old adult would be like. Thanks, but no thanks." Quickly the lady grabbed the two handles on her daughter's wheelchair and headed out the door.

∞∞∞

What is Rett syndrome? From the official correspondence of the Rett organization, it is found to be a "rare genetic neurological disorder that occurs almost exclusively in girls and leads to severe impairments, affecting nearly every aspect of the child's life: their ability to speak, walk, eat, and even breathe easily. The hallmark of Rett syndrome is near constant repetitive hand movements."

In 1966, an Austrian neurologist, Andreas Rett, discovered the disorder after noticing massive abnormalities in some of his female patients. After writing a clinical paper he joined in with a team of other European researchers to do a more intense study that was a continuation from his first initial results. These brilliant researchers found that Rett syndrome is caused by mutations on the X chromosome on a gene called MECP2.

It took until 1981 for American doctors to finally have a label for people with Laura's condition. Sadly, for my sweet sister, this discovery was made when she was at an age when a normal woman would be old enough to graduate high school, land her first job, and go out to a drive-in movie at the Autorama Twins with a fawning boyfriend. In fact, at that time, numbers for children with Rett showed that this syndrome occurs worldwide in 1 of every 10,000 female births, and is even rarer in boys.

⬡⬡⬡

"Chris, come here...and be quiet." My sister Stephanie looked like she was up to no good again.

"What is it Steph?"

"Shhhhhh, be quiet, and slowly look around the

corner."

As I peered from the hallway into our large family room I noticed a shy teenage boy sitting on the couch next to my sister Laura. "His name is Jeff," Stephanie said, "I told him if he wants to go out with me he has to first get approval from my sister Laura."

"Steph, that is so mean!" I said.

She chuckled with her hand over her mouth as we both watched the confused boy awkwardly try to talk to my silent sister. "Hi," he started slowly, "my name is Jeff. Steph tells me you are her older sister Laura. Nice to meet you."

With her hands clenched tight in front of her, Laura started rocking slowly on the couch saying nothing. Jeff held out his hand waiting for her to extend a greeting in return. But there sat Laura, staring forward into space, remaining silent as a statue. And as Jeff continued to move uncomfortably around on the couch I thought to myself, "Poor guy."

This went on for five long minutes until I couldn't take it anymore, "Steph go in there and tell him Laura is handicapped. You are being cruel. He will never want to go out with you after that."

Stephanie hesitated for a moment and laughed. "If he really likes me he will keep trying to get her to talk."

So I went in. "Hey Jeff," I said, "I am Chris, Stephanie's younger brother, and I have seen you in the hallways at school. I am sorry but my sister Laura is mentally slow. She can't respond. Stephanie likes to play practical jokes on people with her. One time she had some of her friends over and Laura started screaming in her bedroom. When her friends asked Steph what that was she looked at them and said, 'Don't worry, it is just the neighborhood serial killer that lives next door.' It scared them half-to-death.'"

Jeff laughed it off and said, "That is what I like about Stephanie, she is so weird."

Laura was a daddy's girl, my father considered her well-being his responsibility. Not only would he keep feeding her at the dinner table long after the rest of us kids were done eating, small bite after small bite, but he never gave up hope for a cure. It was his voice she responded to. He would come into the room and say, "Hey Laura, how are you girl?" She would crinkle her eyes and blow out a small amount of pent-up air from her lungs as her rock got faster.

She knew her dad.

Sometimes he would have all of us sing her favorite songs to her, like "Little Laura Lee and Tiny Bubbles by Don Ho." But when we all sang "I Love to Laugh" something inside her brain fired. Like an old Chevy truck trying to crank over and come alive, Laura's eyes sparked. For a short few seconds you could catch a smile—Laura actually smiled. It wasn't a full wide-awake smile, but it was a faint far-away smile like she was holding a secret only she knew. As if she was trying to tell us all that a better day was coming.

Laura was also my father's partner in crime. When he wanted to get a reaction from my friends at the dinner table he would feed Laura some of the messiest food he could find. The worst of all was watermelon. After each bite of the pink fruit my sister would drool the juice like a waterfall. You couldn't help but look at the chunky liquid that oozed out from her mouth, and as Laura chewed my dad acted like he didn't notice the large, goopy mess she made. He would tie a big towel around her neck and to the surprise of my friends they would gawk as she would slobber and spit. They didn't want to be rude so they didn't say a thing, but my sisters and I couldn't hold in the hilarity.

My dad's bible was filled with prayers for Laura. His favorite verses were dated alongside prayers of petition concerning her, "Lord please heal Laura." Again and again, a father's longing for the health of his girl was recorded. Days, months and years he wrote his requests for his dear girl to have a normal life.

No answer. And then, tragically, his life was cut short.

⟨⟩⟨⟩⟨⟩⟨⟩

Rett syndrome shows no mercy. The body's slow decline under the wicked spell of a few rebellious genes never relents. As the years pass, a person's teeth decay and start to fall out. The muscles in the arms and legs atrophy making a wheelchair a necessary home. Eyes continue to cross, hair grays, hands remain bound in a vice-like grasp, and shoulders start to slump and slouch.

Little Laura Lee she remains.

Years of motherly care is what kept Laura alive. Changing diapers, administering pills, wheeling her in and out of bed has become my mom's faithful daily routine for 60 years. A true servant.

But is it worth it?

Is it worth it to keep someone alive who can't talk back? Sure her brain functions, it sputters and spits, but for what? To run bodily functions? To keep the lungs breathing and heart pumping? Is that really living?

Is Peter Singer, the moral philosopher from Princeton right when he postulates, sitting smugly in his Ivy League office, that some people are inherently "defective"? Is Laura Lee a "defective" human, not fit to waste the resources we normal humans need? Is he right when he says, "not all persons are humans, and some humans are definitely not persons"? And is he also right when he quips that "an adult chimpanzee can exhibit more self-consciousness, more personhood, than a new-born human infant"? Should my sweet sister Laura be compared to a chimp?

Maybe a few mutations on a select group of genes is enough to no longer consider life, life. Did we misplace our love for a sister who is silent?

PART TWO

Life in heaven comes down to numbers.

And when you pause to think about it, the numbers that go into freeing a lost soul from eternal condemnation include some calculations that are quite staggering. Taking an educated guess, there have been at least 600 billion people that have existed over a period of 10,000 years, all of whom were the product of a single sperm cell and egg cell joining to be mingled with the breath of God to form a single human life. The average time span for that one individual soul is 70 years, or 80 if a person has enough strength, so says Moses in Psalm 90. And included in each year is 365.5 days in which a person must make very serious diurnal decisions that they are morally accountable for.

If one, just one of those choices on any particular day is willfully intended to miss the mark of God's holy requirement of perfection, to him or her who chooses to go astray, that singular action is considered to be a sin. Sin, in its essence, and contrasting it to God's holy unblemished standing, demands a severe measure of judgment. In other words, when sin occurs, wrath is required.

Both personal experience and the inner conscience testify to the fact that the act of sin is committed in each of our lives numerous times each day. If we were to apply a conservative estimation saying that sin occurs on average with 10 daily trespasses that would then bring us to a total of 3,655 times individual trespasses are committed per year. A lifetime of sinning adds up to 260,000 infractions which in turn require a mountain of a ransom payment.

Now, here is where the numbers explode, take that 260,000 and multiply it by 600 billion and you are dealing with some devastating eternal numbers. Damnation deserved for collective mankind is a staggering debt.

And yet in one man's volunteer death, the debt was paid. "I am forced to restore what I did not steal," so says the Psalmist. Eternal wrath was swallowed by the infinite being, and so those who have been kept in chains awaiting damnation are miraculously afforded the opportunity to be set free by that one perfect man. The key that unlocks the rusty cage was found.

And look! Look! In Laura's clenched fist there lies a small, shining, golden key dipped in blood.

"But I'm gonna break - I'm gonna break my -

I'm gonna break my rusty cage and run.

Yeah, I'm gonna break - I'm gonna break my -

I'm gonna break my rusty cage and run."

(Rusty Cage, Johnny Cash)

It took me just two quick blinks, a solid rubbing of the eyes with the bony knuckle of my right index finger, and now, for the very first time in my life, I was utterly, completely, wide awake. Normally after a long nap my mind operates agonizingly slow; like rousing my fat dog out of a heavy afternoon slumber, I am always a tad bit groggy. But not this time. It was as if someone dusted out the cobwebs and dirt between my ears, gave me a stiff shot of caffeine, and pulled me up by both shoulders with a firm double-fisted grab.

I remember everything in exquisite detail: I was out in the woods on a snowy morning, the huge trees around me towered like massive wooden beams holding up the roof of an outdoor cathedral while flakes of soft snow cascaded down. The air was crisp and cool, and each breath of the fresh draft of air I took made it harder and harder to breathe. It was a strange feeling; the more I inhaled the less air I took in. My lungs refused entrance. I had to stop.

I found a large oak near me to lean on, and as I raised my arm to steady myself against the rough bark something stabbed my chest with an invisible sharp blade to the left side of my heart. My knees buckled and I instantly dropped on the soft snow. With my head leaning back and my eyes looking up, it was as if the whole world went into a slow-motion fade. As each falling flake tumbled and twirled toward me, I could detect each intricate detail and pattern on the dancing white crystals. A bright blue blur then started to expand. My dog licked me with his hot breath and then nuzzled his warm head next to my face. I tried for one last swallow of air.

Nothing.

⊃⊂⊃⊂⊃

I was told that a good death was like a normal night of sleep. You shut your eyes, lay your head down on the soft familiar pillow, and then the next thing you know you wake up the next morning in a brand new room not remembering a thing about the previous night's sleep. Easy peasy!

I wouldn't describe death like that at all.

The best way I can explain it that it reminds me of the time I went scuba diving with my scuba class in the cold waters of a Northern Ohio limestone quarry in early March. It was a cold day, just above freezing. The sun was trying to peek out, but the heavy gray line of low morning clouds did all they could to keep the bright sun's magnificence at bay.

The first order of business when our class arrived at the water's edge was to put on our thick claustrophobic wetsuits. We were told that the wetsuit was made to keep a person's body temperature at even 98 degrees even while they were submerged under frigid 38-degree ice-water. I wasn't comforted. And I did not want to go swimming. But since this was our final exam in the scuba class, I had no other choice.

"One, two, three!" Holding my partner's hand with my right, and keeping a good grip over my mask with my left, we took the plunge. Splash! Down we went. Our instructor told us we had a good thirty minutes of swim time to go the full 140 feet down to explore the bottom of the quarry. There were supposed to be sunken boats and old grain silos we could explore—a scuba diver's paradise. But in such cold and inky-black waters, it felt more like a mission to go explore the entrance into hell. I will never forget the anxious feeling I had when we descended into those gloomy foreboding waters. You could only see a few feet in front of you, and no more.

We didn't find any of the sunken boats or grain silo, and after a good ten minutes of uneventful swimming, my breathing buddy motioned to me, "Let's go back up! I am running out of oxygen." He was nervous so his heavy breathing used up the oxygen in his tank fast. So, we grabbed hands again and used the rubber flippers on our feet to slowly ascend.

It was strange, I didn't notice it on the way down, but the higher we got the warmer the water became. Even through the heavy padding of the wetsuit the change in the temperature was pleasantly surprising. When we swam up to around the forty-foot line there was something inviting about the water, you could see the rays of the sun piercing holes through the thick liquid darkness. A warm umbrella of heat was radiating across the body of water, and to our amazement, we were now being welcomed by a bright yellow glow upon the surface. The higher we went the more you could see, breathing became easier, and fish could be spotted everywhere. We escaped the mouth of hell.

I will never forget the sensation of breaking the surface of the water. I took off my mask, inhaled fresh air, and was stunned by the golden ball shining superior over the fleeting distant clouds. Wow, the sun was so bright! So bright! And the sky was so blue! Heavenly blue!

That is what death is like.

I was awake alright. But not like before. Oh no, nothing like before. No longer was I submerged under the dark emotions of my murky soul. Everything was so bright, like a blazing torch through polished clear glass. How do I describe something that has no language or words to describe? All I can do is try.

The first thing I noticed was my hands. I had the same hands, but they had no blemishes, no sunspots or deep wrinkles, no scars, and no dirt under the nails. And they felt strong, really, really strong. They were still my hands, but not the hands I knew.

I bent over and I picked up a rock to see if my hands felt familiar. It was a small gray rock and I held it loosely in the palm of my hand. It was like holding a feather. Running it between my thumb and forefinger I could feel every curve, ripple, and ridge on the rock. It was strange they way l could sense everything, I felt color and density, warm and cold, all in a few seconds. But there really were no seconds, everything just was.

I rubbed a bit harder on the surface and the rock started polishing to a bright purple hue, like the old cat-eye marbles my mom would buy me for Christmas. My hands were actually polishing this rock to a fine finish in no time. I wanted to hang on to it as a keepsake—a reminder to prove I wasn't going mad. But right before I went to put it into my pocket, I looked up and then realized that I didn't need any reminder of a momentary memory because polished rock was everywhere.

Gleaming stones of translucent colors could be seen in every direction I looked and walked. Large boulders of sapphire, ruby and a bright green emerald lined a shimmering blue creek that flowed merrily by. Looking into the flowing crystal water I could spot other bright rocks of every color and size under the surface. Was that a fish? A glittery silver trout kept jumping from the surface as if he was welcoming me to this new world. Surprisingly, the large fish wasn't trying to swim away, he was not scared of my presence. He was confident and sure, begging me to catch him.

I turned around and a thick green carpet of grass was everywhere. White puffy clouds floated in a soft blue sky. Trees were dancing in the distance swaying to the movements of a friendly warm breeze. Were the trees singing? Or were they clapping their hands? Wait, yes, they were singing!

I held my breath to listen.

I've never been known to be much of a musician, but I knew the song that was being sung. Why would trees be singing *that* song? Softly padding across the lush verdure, I moved closer to hear. The sound was clear, strong and it carried with it a sweet melodic joy. And the words, they were more than familiar, they actually seemed to be a part of me. Whoever it was that was singing, they were in the middle of the song,

"Then there's the kind.

That can't make up their mind…"

I know that song! But it can't be. I had to get closer. A few more steps and I was almost fully under the giant oak's enormous canopy of soft orange and yellow leaves. The song continued and it was then I realized I was wrong. The musical performance wasn't coming from the trees, but I noticed that there was a person sitting down on the other side at the base of the oak with their back to me. Here was the one who was singing!

I looked closer and I saw a beautiful woman with a head full of light golden locks. She had her head resting comfortably against the soft bark. With effortless ease, the happy notes flowed from her enchanting voice,

"When things strike me as funny

I can't hide it inside

And squeak as the squeakelers do

I've got to let go with a ho ho ho

And a ha ha ha too"

I couldn't help myself, the music took over and I felt compelled to join in the chorus with the signing cherub under the tree,

"We love to laugh

Loud and long and clear

We love to laugh

So everybody can hear"

I startled the person sitting, she stopped singing and turned my way.

"I'm so sorry, please don't stop. I love that song and your voice." I bowed my head to hide my embarrassment. I felt like I was an unwelcome intruder on a lovely dream. But this wasn't a dream.

"Chris! It's you! My dear brother Chris. I've been waiting for you. I've been sent here to wait by the Celebration Tree to be the first one to greet you! I asked if I could."

I lifted my head and walking toward me in a flowing white robe, wrapped in an assorted chain of wildflowers, was a tall, elegant woman with bronze flawless skin. She smiled a large brilliant smile with arms outstretched. I looked deep into this wonderful smiling face standing before me and I was completely taken aback. I could not believe my eyes. It just couldn't be.

"Laura Lee, it's you!"

∞∞∞∞

With two perfect arms, my very own sister Laura held me tight in a strong warm hug. My older sister was like a goddess. She lifted me up with ease and set me down softly, saying, "Chris, I have so much to show you." Pointing off to a gleaming city in the far distance she said,

"I can't wait to watch your face as you see him."

"See who?"

Laura looked at me and hugged me again, "It is so good to see you!"

She grabbed my hand in hers and we started to run. "Sing it with me, Chris! The melody reminds me of our home on the other side."

So she led me in the joyous chorus as we floated across a meadow of unending beauty and wonder,

"I love to laugh
Loud and long and clear
I love to laugh
It's getting worse every year"

She slowed a bit and led me toward a mysterious tree. "Chris, we are allowed to eat this now. Its taste is amazing. And it is abundant up here." Reaching high Laura grabbed a juicy red fruit I had never seen before. It looked delicious.

"What is it, Laura?"

"Try it and you tell me."

I grabbed the large fruit in both of my hands and took a small bite. A flood of energy instantly shot through me, warm, vibrant life. "It is the fruit of life! Take a bigger bite than that," Laura laughed, "We have nothing to worry about anymore." I opened my mouth wide and chomped, a thick sweet juice rolled down my cheek. I wiped the excess off my chin with the back of my hand.

"You know who you remind me of?" Laura said to me as a mischievous smile flashed across her radiant face.

"No, who?" I wondered as more of the juice trickled down the side of my mouth.

"You look just like me in my earlier days. Remember when dad fed me watermelon and everyone, especially Gina, couldn't stop laughing? And guess what? One time, I heard you laughing at me the loudest."

"I'm so sorry Lara, I didn't mean it. I was a foolish

kid." Laura did not look offended. Her face showed just the opposite, she was delighted. And in a spontaneous response of joy, she tousled my hair and said, "Chris that is what little brothers do. No worries."

∽∽∽∽

"Five more minutes until we arrive, everyone is waiting to see you. The most incredible people will be there."

I remained silent, still remembering how I often mistreated and mostly ignored Laura's existence for over sixty-five long years. And here she was, enjoying being in my presence, laughing and forgetting. How could she forget?

"Chris, what is it? You look at bit sad. Aren't you excited to get to the Great City? It is like nothing you have ever imagined." Laura looked deep into my face, trying to cheer me up. "What is on your mind?"

"Laura, aren't you angry at me? And for that

matter, don't you want to get back at everyone who saw you only as a useless cripple, an inconvenience? Look at you now, you did not deserve the bad treatment you received for the majority of your sad life."

Laura grabbed both of my shoulders and with a look of intensity she said to me, "Life? What life? You haven't yet seen life in all its fullness. What we lived on the other side wasn't life, it was mere survival. Just wait until you see life, THE LIFE, in person. His singular presence turns time, and sorrow for that matter, back on its head. Just wait and keep eating that fruit, it will clear your mind of regret and self-pity."

Scratching my head, I responded, "Laura I just don't understand. Don't you feel robbed?"

"Chris, you taught the Bible most of your life, my joy shouldn't surprise you at all. Didn't you believe what you yourself taught? Remember what Paul wrote in Corinthians? 'Death has been swallowed up in victory.' What do you think that means? Was Paul just whistling in the wind or was he serious?"

I didn't know what to say.

"Chris, little brother, my pain has been swallowed, reversed, turned upside down. When you swallow food it adds back proportional life. Think back—the more you eat, the stronger you get. In a very strange way, I feel like I am the lucky one because my suffering has brought me proportional joy. In some ways, I feel sorry for those who never understood the fellowship that was found in my Lord's suffering. The fruit it bears in this world we now live in cannot be compared."

The city was close now. You could hear the laughter and feel the warmth radiate from its shining walls.

◦◦◦◦

"Look!" Laura said, "Do you see him? He is running toward us."

"Laura, I can't see that far. You sure have some

good eyesight." As I was squinting off into the distance, I placed my hand over my eyes to try to reduce the sharp glare of the shining city. All I could make out was a blurry figure of a man in white heading quickly in our direction.

Laura smiled and said, "Oh yeah, you haven't been here that long. But don't worry, your eyesight will steadily improve along with your strength and hearing. He is fast, so get ready, he should be here at any moment now.

The large figure was getting closer and following him was at least one hundred other people. They were all singing, some were shouting, others were chanting praises of the one they were following with joy.

Laura grabbed my hand tight—wow did she have strong and sure hands—and with uncontainable excitement said, "You have to be able to see him now. You can't miss him. Isn't he just marvelous?"

I did see him. The one who paid my ransom.

The face I was waiting to behold my whole life

was more wonderful than I expected. Marvelous, sublime, and kind. And look! My dad was right behind him with tears of joy falling down his face.

∞∞∞

My redeemer shows mercy. The body I once had, with aching bones and failing heart, has been swallowed up in glory. As the years and centuries pass in the other world, I found that a person grows younger, stronger. The muscles in the arms and legs are indestructible; a body that once was a tent becomes a permanent home. Eyes now see for hundreds of miles, hair glows gold, hands remain strong, and shoulders stand erect and strong.

Little Laura Lee is little no more.

My Lord kept Laura alive the whole time. While she was locked in her rusty cage, no one but Him even noticed the priceless soul that was waiting to be set free. Our Lord's broken body on the cross sprung the lock that was keeping her bound, and his spilled red blood was the key that opened the cage.

But was it worth it?

Ask Laura Lee that question. She will answer it for you! For her, being bound 60 years in a rusty cage is not comparable to the freedom that eternity promises for those that Christ loves.

What does the "great" Peter Singer have to say about this? There is only one who is great—and Peter Singer is not he! And even his "defective" body theory is no match for the powerful reality of Christ's "effective" grace. The resources we normal humans fight to obtain down here are like mere trifles compared to the scrumptious fruit of life that is waiting for us on the other side. Is Peter Singer right when he says, "not all persons are humans"? In some ways, he is naively accurate because once you take a glimpse of Laura Lee in glory, you will see that immortality turns a mere human into a mighty being fit to walk the streets of gold.

A few hours of hanging on the cross was enough. His love was not misplaced, and as a result, my sister is not going to be relegated to silence. In fact, if you listen closely, you might just hear her singing,

"The more I laugh, the more I fill with glee
And the more the glee
The more I'm a merrier me, it's embarrassing
The more I'm a merrier me"

www.ingramcontent.com/pod-product-compliance
Lightning Source LLC
Chambersburg PA
CBHW060501130626
46555CB00017B/2823